RED

SHAM
POO

To Emma – SG

For the little white duck that lives in Windsor – NL

First published in Great Britain in 2002 by Bloomsbury Publishing Plc
38 Soho Square, London, W1D 3HB

A CIP catalogue record of this book is available from the British Library
ISBN 0 7475 5061 1

Designed by Sarah Hodder
Printed in Hongkong by Wing King Tong

1 3 5 7 9 10 8 6 4 2

Mucky Duck

Sally Grindley

Illustrations by Neal Layton

Oliver Dunkley had a pond in his garden, and on that pond lived Mucky Duck.

Mucky Duck was supposed to be white,
and sometimes she was, but mostly she wasn't.
And this is why...

FLOUR
PEPPE
Strawberry Jam

Mucky Duck liked cooking. Pouring and mixing, rolling and shaping.

O you Mucky Duck!

Mucky Duck liked football. Dribbling and tackling, shooting and diving.

O you Mucky Duck!

Mucky Duck liked painting. Dipping
and sponging, squirting and splattering.

PINK

RED

O you Mucky Duck!

Mucky Duck liked gardening. Digging and weeding, planting and sowing.

O you Mucky Duck!

So once every week Mucky Duck had to have a bath.

Wash, wipe, rub, scrub.

And Mucky Duck didn't like that.

Who's a clean Mucky Duck then!

But not for long!

O you Mucky Duck!
Mucky Duck
Sally Grindley
Neal Layton

SOAP